God Gave Us Christmas

by Lisa Tawn Bergren · art by David Hohn

WATERBROOK
PRESS

GOD GAVE US CHRISTMAS

Hardcover ISBN 978-1-4000-7175-3
eBook ISBN 978-0-307-73085-5

Text copyright © 2006 by Lisa Tawn Bergren

Illustrations copyright © 2006 by David Hohn

Published in the United States by WaterBrook, an imprint of the Crown Publishing Group, a division of Penguin Random House LLC, New York.

WATERBROOK® and its deer colophon are registered trademarks of Penguin Random House LLC.

Library of Congress Cataloging-in-Publication Data
Bergren, Lisa Tawn.
  God gave us Christmas / Lisa Tawn Bergren ; illustrations by David Hohn.— 1st ed.
       p. cm.
  Summary: Mama Bear explains to Baby Cub how God gave Christmas to the world.
  ISBN 1-4000-7175-5
[1. Christmas—Fiction. 2. God—Fiction. 3. Bears—Fiction.]   I. Hohn, David, 1974-   , ill.
II. Title.
PZ7.B452233Go 2006
[E]—dc22
                                        2006008584

Printed in the United States of America
2018

25 24 23 22 21 20 19 18 17

To our godchildren — Joel, Eden, Hope;

and in memory, Madison Grace —

always remember that

God gave each of YOU Christmas!

"Mama,"
Little Cub asked one night.
"Who 'vented Christmas?
Was it Santa?"

"No," Mama Bear said. "God invented Christmas.
God gave us Christmas."

"Is God more important than Santa?"

"Oh yes, much more important!"
Mama said with a smile.

The next morning,
Little Cub sleepily climbed into her lap.
"Can we go find Santa, Mama?
He lives 'round here someplace, I think."

"Hmm. Santa is hard to find," said Mama.
"But we can go find God. God is everywhere."

"Yahoo!" cried Little Cub. "I didn't know we could find God!"

"Oh yes," Mama said. "We can always find God."

Little Cub looked over her shoulder and whispered, "Can we leave them at home?"

"Yes, Papa will watch the little ones. You and I can go alone."

"We will go find God?
I will see how he gave us Christmas?"

"Yes, Little Cub,
you shall see how God gave us Christmas."

The next morning
Little Cub and Mama filled their packs,
kissed their family good-bye
and set off to find God
and see how he gave them Christmas.
They walked to the top of one mountain…

And down the next…

And up another mountain…
where they set up camp.

Little Cub was so, so tired that she went right to sleep.

But Mama nudged her while it was still dark!
"M-Mama? Why're you wakin' me up?"

"Because it's *God*, Little Cub. Come see!"

"What is *that*?" Little Cub asked in wonder as she watched the dancing lights in the sky.

"That is God at work, Little Cub.

He sent his only Son as a baby
so that we would know light from dark.
Jesus is the light of the world.
Jesus is how God gave us Christmas."

The next day they arrived at a huge lake.
All at once, with a mighty roar,
a chunk of ice cut away from the cliff
and fell into the sea!

"What is *that*?" Little Cub asked,
covering her ears and leaning into Mama.

"That is God, Little Cub.
He's so powerful he can command the water to freeze
and the glacier to melt. He is mightier than any king on earth.
And because he is all-powerful, he made Jesus King of all kings."

"But Jesus was just a baby!
How could he be a king?"

"All kings begin as babies.
God knew we would need
someone we could touch
and see and smell—"

Mama paused to sniff Little Cub's
neck, making her giggle—
"to understand just how much
he loved each one of us."

Mama awoke Little Cub again before the sun came up.
She pointed to the east, at a star that changed
from green to red to green again
and shot out in many points.

"Is 'at God again?"
Little Cub asked,
rubbing her eyes.

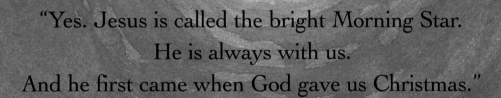

"Yes. Jesus is called the bright Morning Star.
He is always with us.
And he first came when God gave us Christmas."

"But what about Santa?" Little Cub asked.
"Did God give us Santa?"

"Santa Claus reminds us about many
good things like generosity and care.
But it is God and Jesus that we celebrate most come Christmas.
We always want to thank *God* for giving us Christmas."

On the way home, Mama Bear stopped by a tiny flower peeking up from the hard, frozen ground. "Oh, you are too early, little flower," she said.

"Little Cub, Jesus is like this flower—God in our world. Living where you wouldn't expect him, surprising us! Christmas is a lot about surprises."

"Mm-hmm, like *presents*!"

"Yes! Jesus is the best present of all. And God would've given us that present, even if it was only for you."

"Only for me?"

"Only for you, Little Cub. God gave *you* Christmas."

Mama and Little Cub came upon a church,
glowing with warm light. Soft voices reached
out to them, singing.

"What're they singin', Mama?"

"About the night God first gave us Christmas,
when Jesus was born.
Tomorrow is Christmas day!"

"Would Jesus have come for mean ol' Maggie the Moose or grumpy ol' Frankie the Fox?" Little Cub whispered.

"Maggie, Frankie, any of us. Jesus is a present for everyone, grumpy or happy, mean or kind. God gave us *all* Christmas."

Little Cub was glad to be back at home that night,
in her cozy bed. "Thanks for showing me God, Mama."

"There isn't anything I'd rather do,
sweet child," she said with a kiss.
"Nigh-Night."

Little Cub went to sleep and dreamed of bright stars
and Northern Lights, of a King born as a tiny baby,
angels singing over him,…

And woke up to Christmas!
"Yahoo!" she cried. "God gave us Christmas! AGAIN!"